Adventures of the
Bubble Kids

Book Two: Juneau, Alaska

Paula Shue Winfrey
Illustrated by Ashley L. Voltmer

Amazing Things Press

Book design by Julie L. Casey

ISBN 978-1949830774

Printed in the United States of America.

For more information, visit

www.amazingthingspress.com

Chapter One – Snow Days

The alarm went off and I jumped out of bed like a rocket. I had waited weeks for this day and now it had finally arrived. This was the day my reading group was going to present our reader's theater project about the story of Balto, the heroic sled dog. We had worked for two long months researching the history of Balto.

I was the narrator and had been practicing my lines every night before bed. Heck, I practiced so much I could read everyone else's lines too. If I do say so myself, I'm the most enthusiastic reader in our group.

I rushed around getting ready. Dressed in my lucky outfit, I looked in the mirror and gave myself a big thumbs up. *Lookin' sharp, my man*, I thought to myself. Grabbing my backpack, I glanced to make sure I had my script inside. Check.

I was ready to roll!

I raced out of my room and down the stairs. It was quieter than usual, but that was okay by me. Less interruptions to deal with. I was going to be the first one out the door and at the bus stop. Outta my way, people! Reading star coming through!

I grabbed an apple off the table and headed for the hall closet to find my coat. I was anxious to get to school and look at my script one last time before we performed. This day was going to be epic.

I opened the front door and just stood there with my mouth hanging open. *Are you kidding me?* I thought. This must be some horrible joke. As far as I could see there was nothing but miles of snow. Snow covering everything in sight. Not the type of snow I would be able to shovel away in a few minutes. This was Snowmagedden. This was snow up to my waist. I knew what this probably meant.

Dejected, I closed the door and thought about what I was going to be missing today. My big moment was not going to happen like I had planned. It was then I realized no one in our house was anywhere to be seen. I searched room by room and did not find my family; it felt like they'd been abducted by aliens. Why wasn't anyone else up yet?

I went straight to my parents' room and peeked in the door. There they were, just sleeping away as if it weren't the biggest disaster to happen in my life. Our golden retriever, Baxter, was stretched across his dog bed on the floor next to my mom. He didn't even budge when he saw me, and Baxter is always the first one up in the morning. This was the worst and weirdest day combined.

Feeling sorry for myself, I went back downstairs, laid on the couch, and turned on the TV. There it was. Scrolling across the screen was the sad announcement that school was closed today. It was officially a snow day.

Funny thing is, I would usually be in hog heaven to have a snow day. Snow days rule! But today this snow was ruining everything. No one would see how hard I worked to be ready for my big performance. No one would hear how interesting Balto was. No one would learn about the sled dog teams that became heroes way back in history. No one cared but me, I thought as I drifted off to sleep.

I woke suddenly to the sounds of my family and the smells of breakfast cooking. Wait a minute! Maybe I'd been dreaming. Maybe it was just now time to get up. I scrambled off the couch and hurried into the kitchen. Mom was flipping a batch of pancakes, and Dad was setting the table.

"Hey honey, were you surprised about the snow day?" Mom asked as she set a plate of pancakes in front of me.

Rats. It was real.

"Yeah," I said, "and not in a good way."

"Oh, that's right. I forgot about your big reading day," Mom replied, giving me a hug. "I'm sure you'll get the chance to tell your class about Malto very soon."

"Mom! The dog's name is Balto." I reminded her, running out of patience about this whole thing.

"I'm sorry, Bear," Dad chimed in. "I know your performance means a lot to you. We'll just have to make the best of it today." I was having trouble seeing how this could be the best of anything.

My younger brother, Jared, came rushing into the kitchen.

"Wow! Did you see all that snow out there? It's a mountain!" he proclaimed as he sat down to breakfast.

"Yes, sweetie, it's a lot of snow," Mom agreed, serving up a pile of syrup-covered pancakes for him. "But Bear is not as thrilled as you are with this new development."

"What?" Jared exclaimed, "How are you not happy about a day off from school, Bear? This is the best thing ever. Don't you want to go out and play in the snow all day?"

"No," I replied.

Jared looked at Mom and Dad, shrugged his shoulders, and attacked his stack of pancakes. They knew how I felt. I shuffled upstairs to my room to sulk.

Chapter Two – A Great Idea

It didn't take very long before I stopped moping around. I stood looking out my bedroom window and saw some of the neighbor kids already goofing around in the snow. Some were building snowmen. Some were making snow angels. But most were sliding around on their sleds in their driveways or on the few hills in our neighborhood.

Like it or not, I had to admit that I did want to play in the snow. Jared was right. I love snow days in the winter, which meant an extra break from school. Did I want to waste this day feeling crummy about missing my performance and lose out on playing in the snow? No way.

"Hey, Jared!" I hollered down the steps, "Still want to go outside?" No response. I searched around the house for him until I saw the heap of scarves, gloves, and hats lying on the floor in front of the hall closet.

Someone in a hurry had already dug through the winter clothes.

Opening the curtain, I saw Jared and Jillian out in the backyard piling up snowballs. I knew they were waiting on me to come join them and have our traditional snowball fight. It was always Jared against me and Jillian. She was my sidekick.

"Mom! I'm heading out to play in the snow!" I could hear her voice from somewhere telling me to bundle up and have fun as I rushed out the door. But not before Baxter nosed his way past me to get in on the action. "Hey buddy, are you ready to plow through that snow?" I asked my furry best friend. Baxter wagged his tail and took off, making a dog-shaped path as he went.

The snowball stockpile Jared and Jillian had made was mighty impressive. I hurried to roll some snowballs of my own so we could get on with the battle.

"Jillian, are you ready to be my teammate and take Jared down?" She nodded and smiled as I loaded up an old sand bucket with as many snowballs as it could hold. Jillian grabbed a handful, too. She rushed over to hide behind the trash barrel with me. It was one of the best spots we had to take cover.

Jared decided to scrunch down behind Mom's red van. He filled an empty flowerpot with his snowballs.

"Everybody ready?" Jared yelled from his fortress. "On the count of three. One. Two. Three!"

We all popped out from our hiding places and started chucking snowballs at each other. It was a free for all. Jillian was supposed to be on my team, but she just ran around like her hair was on fire, throwing snowballs at anything in sight—the car, the house, and poor ol' Baxter who didn't appreciate a snout full of snow. It was lots of fun, but we ran out of snowballs way too soon. Time to think of something else to do. I had the perfect idea.

"Hey, guys! I thought of something." I announced. "I wasn't able to do my reading performance today, but you two could help me act it out!"

I realized that we had the snow, the sled, and a dog. This could be awesome. "Let me tell you about Balto the dog, and we'll pretend to be part of his story. Are you in?"

"Heck, yeah!" Jared exclaimed. Jared is always in. He loves anything that involves an adventure. And

Jillian goes along with practically everything we come up with.

"Who's Balto?" she asked.

"Balto is the coolest dog ever. That's who he is."

I realized what I had said as soon as I looked over at Baxter, who gave me a wounded look. "Well, besides you, Baxter."

Jared and Jillian sat on a big mound of snow, ready to listen as I told them the story of Balto. "A really long time ago in the winter of 1925 at a place called Nome, Alaska, a lot of people were getting sick with a terrible disease called diphtheria," I began.

"There was a lifesaving antitoxin in Nome, but it had gone bad and couldn't be used. The town leaders had to figure out how to find more antitoxin, but nothing was close by. Getting this medicine to the place it was needed was going to be super hard. The people in that area got their supplies mostly by ship or boat, but icy water had made that impossible. People were dying, and the only way to get the antitoxin to Nome was by dog sled.

"Time out," said Jared, "What's an antitoxin?"

"I'm glad you asked!" I said, ready to use my newfound knowledge. I was feeling quite brainy.

"It's a special medicine that gets rid of certain kinds of germs that make people sick."

"Hmm," Jared said. "Do you drink it?"

"Nope," I told him. "You get a shot from a doctor."

"Ew. I hate shots." Jillian piped in, making a big frowny face. She really did. I don't like them either, but she starts screaming if she sees a needle.

"Don't worry, Jillian," I assured her, "No shots for you today."

"Now back to the story," I continued. "Things were getting worse quickly and there was no time to spare."

"Couldn't they just fly the antitoxin in a plane to help the people in Nome faster?" interrupted Jared.

"Believe it or not, back then planes weren't everywhere like they are now, but the harsh winter conditions made it nearly impossible to even try to fly."

"Whoa," Jared said, "that's awful."

"Yes, it was awful. The town decided the quickest way to get the antitoxin was by dog sled teams."

"That sounds like fun!" Jillian said enthusiastically.

"I guess it could be if things weren't so serious, but people were becoming very sick and some were even dying. They had to work fast," I told them. "The 674-mile trip would usually take twenty-five days to make, but the antitoxin lasted for only six days. Things seemed impossible.

"Here's where it gets exciting." I explained. "Most of the dog teams were experienced, but it was one of the coldest winters in 20 years, so the teams would have to cross dangerous ice-covered ground. The 20-pound package of antitoxin had to stay wrapped up so it wouldn't freeze. It was so cold that some of the mushers got frostbite."

"Wait a minute, wait a minute!" Jared hollered out. "What's a musher? That's a weird word. And how about frostbite? I never heard of that either."

"Good questions, little brother. You've asked the right guy."

I explained that mushers were the people who trained and kept the dog sled teams moving in the right direction. They took care of the dogs too. It was a big job to keep as many as sixteen dogs all hitched together while they ran over snow and ice-covered places as fast as they could.

"Frostbite is when skin gets too cold and causes painful damage. That's why we bundle up in warm clothes when it's very cold outside."

"Man, I don't ever want to get frostbite!" Jared said, shaking his head.

"Me either, but these mushers were trying to hurry as quickly as possible to save lives, so they kept on going even with frostbite.

"No dog sled team was supposed to run more than 100 miles at a time," I continued, "so they had a relay of teams ready to hand off the antitoxin and hurry to the next stop."

"How could they get to Nome in time with a bunch of dog sled teams?" Jared wondered. "Those dogs must run really fast!"

"They ran day and night. Some of the dogs got hurt and died. One musher had to pull the sled himself! Another one's hands froze to the handlebars and the next team's musher had to pour hot water over his hands to get them loose."

Jared and Jillian sat there staring at me, eyes big and waiting to hear what was going to happen next. I paused dramatically. This was almost better than my reader's theater performance was going to be.

My story continued, "Some teams struggled over jagged piles of ice, while others ran over frozen water with big dangerous cracks that the dogs, sleds, and mushers could've fallen into. There was even a part of the trail that one team had to climb eight miles up a mountain to get to. Terrible blizzards were coming in and a musher named Gunnar Kaasen along with his lead dog, Balto, plowed through the snow and ice all night, accidentally missing the hand off to the next team. Once he realized he had gone too far, he just decided to keep going. Suddenly, a big gust of wind turned over his sled and the package of antitoxin flew into a snowbank and was buried in the snow."

"Wait! What?" Jared exclaimed. "How could he find it in the snow during a blizzard?"

"He did the only thing he could, he used his bare hands to dig through the snow until he felt the package. He ended up with frostbite on his hands, but he kept on going. The next musher on the trail thought

Kaasen was late, so he fell asleep waiting for him. Kaasen chose not to wake him up since the dog team was running so well. The team led by Balto, finished the last twenty-five miles, pulling into Nome at 5:30 in the morning. Not one glass vial of antitoxin was broken and after the town got their shots, the disease began to slow down. Many lives were saved."

"Wow," Jared whispered, "that's amazing."

Jillian had fallen asleep leaning on Jared's shoulder. I don't think a three-year old is as interested in the story as I am.

"What happened to Balto?" Jared wondered.

"Balto and one of his dog teammates, Togo, whose team ran the farthest, became famous. Huge crowds came to see them, and the President of the United States at the time, Calvin Coolidge, presented the mushers and their dogs with fancy awards of commendation to show the world how heroic they were.

"Where's Balto now?" Jared asked.

"Little brother, that was a really long time ago. I wish dogs could live that long, but after both Balto and Togo died, they were stuffed by taxidermists and put on display in museums so people today can still see what they looked like back then. There are cool statues of Balto in both New York City's Central Park and downtown Anchorage, Alaska. They named this amazing event, The Great Race of Mercy. Isn't that one of the coolest stories you've ever heard?" I asked.

Jared nodded his head and grinned, looking right at Baxter. He said, "Let's play The Great Race of Mercy right now!"

I was thinking the very same thing.

Chapter Three – Mush!

We found our old snow sled inside the garage and hooked it up to Baxter's collar with a jump rope. Baxter is such a good sport. He lets us play with him and just goes along with our kooky plans.

We put Jillian on the sled with a little backpack full of juice boxes that would be our fake medicine on our fake trip to Nome. After tying more jump ropes to the sled, Jared and I became the dog team mushers and took turns helping Baxter haul Jillian around the yard as fast as we could run. It was lots of fun. Especially for Jillian, who was giggling and trying not to fall off the sled when we would hit a rough patch.

Suddenly I had a grand idea. I ran inside the house to the kitchen and grabbed the bottle of Marvin's Magic Bubbles from the cabinet.

When Jared and Jillian saw what I had in my hand, they gave each other a big high five with excitement.

"Is it time for another adventure?" asked Jared, his eyes big with hope.

"Maybe." I answered. "It's all up to Baxter."

We unhooked our faithful pal from the sled. I poured some bubble solution on a spot I had cleared off the driveway and waited to see what Baxter would do.

He wandered over to the bubble water and began to sniff at it. Just like before, it stuck to his nose and he shook his head back and forth to get it off. As he snorted and snuffled, the solution began to grow into a bubble. We all hurried over to watch. Before our eyes, the magic happened. The bubble had gotten so large that it completely covered over us and lifted us gently off the ground. This time we weren't scared. Instead, we were super pumped up about going on another amazing adventure!

As we floated higher into the air, our house appeared smaller and smaller. Our neighborhood friends looked like tiny ants from way up there. Of course, they couldn't see us as we caught a breeze and moved farther away. Up, up we climbed until our house was out of sight.

"Look at the snow everywhere!" hollered Jared. "It's like a giant white blanket covering the world." It was incredible. I had never seen so much snow at one time.

Then the deep voice I had hoped to hear began to speak. "We couldn't have picked a better day for an adventure, could we, kids?" Baxter asked excitedly.

The sound of Baxter talking was always such an amazing surprise. I looked him in the eyes and said, "Nice to be on another great adventure with you, buddy!"

Jared and Jillian hugged Baxter and he nuzzled their faces.

"It's going to be a very exciting trip this time," said Baxter. "Can you guess where we'll be going?"

Jared's eyes lit up and he started humming the Fifty Nifty United States song, then yelled out, "Alaska!"

"Yes, indeed," answered Baxter. "Alaska, the Last Frontier. It's going to be a most adventurous journey."

"Man, Baxter, this is perfect!" I said as my mind was thinking of my cancelled reading project. "I know exactly what I'd like to see, if it's possible."

"I'm way ahead of you, Bear," said Baxter calmly. "I heard about your disappointing day, so I think you will be very pleased by our destination today."

I could hardly believe what I was hearing. I wondered where we were going and hoped that somehow it included a little something to do with good ol' Balto.

We were moving so quickly over the earth below. Most of what we saw was snow-covered land, but we also saw lots of frozen or nearly frozen bodies of water. I could tell we had been following the Missouri River since we left home. It was winding like a big icy snake as we traveled north.

"Look at those big round ice cubes in the river!" shouted Jillian.

I chuckled and answered, "Yep, they sure do look like big ice cubes. Those pieces of ice bounce off each other causing the straight edges to smooth into the round shapes you see. They go 'round and 'round as they float along."

Social Studies has always been my favorite subject in school. I'm pretty good at remembering cool stuff like that.

"You're right, Bear." said Baxter, "Now I've got a challenge for you! Keep an eye out as we follow the river and try to guess how many states we are cruising over."

We looked under our bubble at the rapidly passing ground below us. I knew we were headed northwest, but since we couldn't actually see the border lines between states, I was trying to picture a map of the United States in my head.

A flock of geese was flying right beside us, then suddenly veered away and began to drop down toward a lake we were traveling over. It was so amazing to see the world from this view. Birds are so lucky to do this every single day.

"Ok Baxter, I can tell we're traveling northwest, so we must be going over Nebraska, South Dakota, North Dakota, and Montana. I remember reading that the Missouri River has its start in the Rocky Mountains of Montana. It's the longest river in North America."

"Nicely done, Bear." Baxter replied. "I can tell you've been paying attention in school. We will float over all those states on our way to Alaska."

"Whoa! That's a lot of states," declared Jared. "the U.S. is a lot bigger than I thought. It goes on forever!"

"It does seem like forever," said Baxter, "but soon we will be floating over a whole other country. Do you know what that country is?"

My mind was still picturing a map in my head and I remembered that once we got to Montana, we were going to run out of states and not be in the U.S. anymore. "Hey, Baxter!" I announced excitedly. "I'm pretty sure we're going to travel through Canada, our neighbor to the north. That would be so fantastic!"

"I'm glad you think so," Baxter replied. "Alaska is special because it doesn't physically border any of the other 48 states in North America. We will have to travel through Canada to get to Alaska. Canada is the large country between the United States and Alaska, or our neighbor to the north as Bear likes to say."

"You mean it's not connected to the rest of the United States?" Jared said with disbelief. "Why not?"

I knew a little of Alaska's history from what I learned on my reading project, so I took a stab at answering him. "The land we call Alaska has been a home to native tribes such as the Auke and Taku for thousands of years. It wasn't until explorers traveled from Europe to that area that others became interested in owning it for their own use. There was a big gold discovery in the late 1800s that brought all kinds of people hoping to get rich to the area that's now called Juneau.

"Gold treasure! Cool. Maybe we'll find big ol' gold nuggets while we're there," Jared said with glee.

Baxter chuckled and said, "I don't think we'll have time for gold mining this trip, but maybe next time."

I continued, "Eventually, the United States bought that land for its natural resources and after a long time of being called a territory, it became our 49th state way back in 1959."

"There are 50 states, right?" asked Jared. "So, where's number 50 if it's not connected to the other 48, either? This sounds confusing."

"Well, it can be," I said, "and to make it even more confusing, number 50 is another special state called Hawaii. Like Alaska, the islands of Hawaii are far away from the rest of the main 48 states. It's possible to take a very long drive from home to Alaska, but you'd have to travel across the Pacific Ocean by boat or plane to see Hawaii."

"Wow. It's a good thing we are traveling in style, huh? I'll bet you no one else has taken a bubble to see Alaska before!" Jared said proudly.

"I think you'd win that bet, little brother." I answered, smiling.

Baxter asked us to look down and notice that the Missouri River had ended. Ahead of us were snow-covered mountains as far as our eyes could see. The mountains looked like someone had squished up flat land into a gigantic pile of rocks. I couldn't quit staring at them.

We just enjoyed the view. Soon a very large body of water appeared to the west of where we were. I knew Jared would be majorly excited about this.

"Is that an ocean?" he asked, awestruck. "It's really, really big!"

Baxter replied, "It sure is. You're looking at the Pacific Ocean right now." My eyes searched up ahead and I could see the shoreline, or the edge of where the land and ocean met. It was like that for a long distance. The land below was still mostly covered in snow, but there were patches of green and brown peeking out, too. And many lakes all around.

"We are floating over Canada's west coast as we speak." Baxter announced.

"Fun fact," I said, remembering something I had learned. "Alaska covers as much land as our three largest states: Texas, California, and Montana combined. But Alaska has less people than almost every other state. It's mostly wilderness."

"Wilderness?" Jared said in a nervous voice. "You mean there're wild animals in Alaska?" he asked, trying to wrap his head around this new information. Jillian looked a little scared, too.

Baxter noticed their worried faces and assured us that we'd be alright. "No reason to be scared, kids." He said. "We won't be deep in the wilderness of Alaska this time. Where we're going, we may see some interesting animals, but I promise I won't let you become a snack."

Chapter Four – North to Alaska

"Hang on," Baxter told us. "We're catching a strong wind that will be carrying us to our destination."

Boy, was he ever right about the strong wind! Our bubble began to move faster and faster. We couldn't focus on the ground below us anymore. It was just a blur of movement whizzing by.

"Yahoo!" yelled Jillian over the sound of rushing wind. She was having a blast and the faster we went, the better she liked it.

We were most definitely not home anymore.

The wind up here felt different than it did at our house. Occasionally, we could see a tiny spot that looked like people lived there, but it wasn't much bigger than a couple of houses. It must be hard to get to places when everything is spread so far apart. I'm used to a short trip with Mom or Dad to the store. I don't think it's like that in most of Alaska from what I was seeing below.

The snow-covered mountains beneath us were right next to the ocean. It was very beautiful. We were slowing down and were able to see islands off the edge of the shore. As we got closer, we could see a city nestled between the mountains and the ocean. It was shaped like the curve of the coastline.

"Baxter, it looks like we're coming into a bigger town. Are we getting ready to land?" I asked.

"We are. This city is called Juneau," Baxter answered. "Fun fact about Juneau is that you can't get there by a road, but only by boat or plane."

"Or magic bubble!" Jared replied with a laugh. "But, it doesn't look like it's very crowded with people. What's up with that?"

Baxter chuckled and said, "You've got a sharp eye, Jared. "In fact, Juneau is the second largest city in Alaska. It's also the capital city of Alaska where important decisions about things that affect Alaskans are decided. It has a population, or number of people, of just under 32,000. The town we live in has more than double that number of people, but in a much, much smaller area. It makes our town look a lot more crowded."

We were floating way more slowly now until our bubble took a sharp turn toward the mountains. We all got jostled a little and Jillian lost her balance. She grabbed a hold of Baxter by his tail as he asked us to get ready to land.

I was more than a little worried when I saw that we were coming down into a place covered in trees. One pokey tree branch could bring us down much faster than I wanted to think about. Landing was going to be tricky. I wanted to close my eyes in case it all went terribly wrong, but it was such a beautiful view that I couldn't help but look.

"Don't worry, Bear," Baxter said in his comforting voice. "We're going to be just fine. This bubble isn't going to pop before we land. Trust me." How could I not trust my good ol' Baxter? He was the best dog a kid could have.

We landed safely on a path lined by tall trees that looked as straight as soldiers in formation. Baxter popped the bubble with his nose so we could move around.

"Ok, kids," he began, "it's going to be important to stay close together while we're here. There's lots to see, and it'll be easy to get lost if you wander away. It's very cold here in Juneau just like home, so it's good we all have our winter coats on!" Baxter winked at us and I laughed.

The sound of dogs barking in the distance was getting louder as we walked on the path. Baxter began to bark too. Suddenly a dog appeared from around the bend and was running towards us. Jillian ran to hide behind me, peeking around my leg to watch as the dog got closer. This dog was beautiful. It almost looked like it could be a small wolf. Its fur was a mix of light tan, gray and brown with little bits of black. As it came near us, I could see its eyes were an amazing shade of light blue. Its tail began wagging and Baxter ran to greet it.

The two dogs happily leapt around barking and sniffing like old friends. Finally, Baxter turned to us and said, "Kids, this is my good friend, Ahsoka. We became pals in the animal shelter when we were both puppies and she found her forever home here in Juneau a few years ago."

Ahsoka walked slowly up to us, stretching her nose out to greet us.

"Baxter tells me you are his family and traveled here all the way from Missouri. Welcome to Juneau! It's really nice to meet you," Ahsoka said. I knew the magic of the bubbles could make it possible for dogs to talk, but it was still a shock to hear her saying words to us.

Jillian let go of her grip on my leg and stepped around towards Ahsoka to pet her. Jared and I petted her too. Her fur was even thicker than Baxter's. She looked at us with those light blue eyes and said, "Would you like to see where I live and meet my family?"

Baxter replied, "Of course, Ahsoka. It's always fun to meet new friends. This is Bear, Jared, and Jillian. We like to go on adventures together in a magic bubble."

Ahsoka looked at us and said, "Goodness, a magic bubble! That sounds very exciting, Baxter. I haven't traveled in a magic bubble before. Around here we like to travel by sled."

Did I hear what I think I heard? Did she just say 'sled'?

"Baxter, are we gonna see sled dogs here in

Juneau?" I asked.

"Well, you just met one, Bear." Baxter said. "Ahsoka moved here to join a family of mushers who raise and train sled dogs."

I looked at Ahsoka and felt my adrenaline pumping. I was going to see real live sled dogs today. Suddenly, missing my day at school was the best thing that could possibly have happened.

Chapter Five – A Sled Dog's Life

Ahsoka led us down a long, curved road. The sound of barking dogs was very loud now. I couldn't wait to see them for myself. It was beyond exciting!

As we rounded a turn, we saw a cabin up ahead. Next to the cabin was a large flat area filled with what looked like tiny red houses. Each little red house had a silver food dish attached to the side. Dogs were everywhere. Some were lying on top of their little house, some were inside their house, and some were standing outside their house barking or wagging their tails because they knew strangers were coming.

Ahsoka told us not to be scared. The dogs were friendly and just curious.

"Is it okay if we pet the dogs?" asked Jared.

"My friends love to be petted. Making new friends is one of our favorite things to do, besides running." Ahsoka replied.

The dogs were beautiful. I knew a little about the kinds of dogs that became sled dogs, so it was amazing to see that most looked just like I imagined. I wondered if Balto had been in a sled dog camp like this one back in his day.

We walked around saying hi to all the dogs. I showed Jillian how to hold her hand out so they could come up to us if they wanted. She was a little scared to be around so many dogs at once, but soon most of the dogs were licking her hand and letting us pet them. Their fur was so thick. It must be nice and toasty warm for them since they seem to spend so much of their time outside.

I noticed that dark gray clouds had moved in and it felt even colder than when we first arrived. A sharp wind blew around us and I could sense the weather was changing.

Baxter was happy to be seeing his old friend. He and Ahsoka were walking around visiting while we checked out all the sled dogs. We hadn't seen any other people yet, so I was surprised when a man, a teenage boy, and a girl about Jared's age came out of the cabin and walked over to where we stood.

"Can I help you?" asked the man. They were all dressed in heavy winter clothing and boots like they might be working outside.

"Hi. I'm Bear and this is my brother, Jared, and sister, Jillian. That's our dog, Baxter. We were just walking by and heard all the dogs barking, so we came to see what was going on."

The man looked over at Baxter, who was next to Ahsoka. She barked, then Baxter came up to the man as if to say hello.

"Well, hi to you too, Baxter," said the man. "My name's Noah. It's nice to meet you all. Are you from around here?"

"No, we're just passing through. But it's really cool to be where real sled dogs live," I answered. He introduced us to his son, Liam and daughter, Gemma. Liam smiled and waved hi to us, but Gemma just jammed her mittened hands into the pockets of her puffy red coat and scowled. I could see that she wasn't interested in meeting new people right now.

"If you want the real experience of working at a sled dog camp, I could use your help." Noah said. "A winter snowstorm is coming our way and we need to get some things taken care of before the storm starts." I jumped at the chance.

"Oh, man!" I said. "That would be amazing." I went over to where Baxter was standing and asked him if it was okay to stay and help.

"Of course," Baxter replied quietly, "but we'll need to keep an eye out on the weather, so we don't get stuck in the middle of a snowstorm." The wind had kicked up and felt even colder now. I was so excited to help with the sled dogs, but I was getting a little nervous about how the sky looked.

Noah gave us all chores to help with. I worked with him to put fresh dry straw into the little dog houses.

"I don't think I'd want to be in those little houses when it's so cold." Jared said.

"It might not look like much," answered Noah. "but this straw makes a nice comfy bed for the dogs, and these houses are built off the ground so that they stay plenty warm."

"Their houses are just big enough for them to move around inside, but small enough to hold in their body heat. When they sleep, they often wrap their tails around their nose to trap in the warmth."

"Hey! That's kinda what I do when I'm cold in bed," Jared told him. I laughed when he said that.

Jared shook his head and replied, "Well I mean, I don't have a tail to cover my nose, but I put a blanket up by my face and I breathe in the warm air. Geesh."

Noah smiled. "Yep, that's how it works. Now we need to get the dogs fed. They eat special food with high protein and high fat since they burn so many calories running." Liam carried the container of dog food for Jillian as she scooped it into the dog dishes and watched them gobble it up.

We helped finish the chores with the dogs, and Noah asked us if we'd like to see pictures of the dogs in action.

"Are you kidding?" I asked. "This is like my dream come true!" This day was just getting better and better. Suddenly we heard a door slam nearby.

"I'm sorry," explained Noah, "Gemma is upset with me right now. She helps a lot around the camp and wants to lead the dogs on the sled like Liam and I, but she's just not ready. It can be dangerous and requires so much practice. I told her we'd keep working on it. I just need to give her a little space to cool off."

I felt badly for Gemma. If I lived around the dogs all day, I'd want to lead them on the sled too.

We followed Noah and Liam into their cabin. It was incredible. The round log walls looked exactly like the logs did from the outside. There was a giant fireplace on one wall and on all the other walls hung sled dog pictures and antique sledding equipment.

"How long have you been a musher?" I asked.

"I'm the fourth generation in a family of mushers here in Juneau. Sled dogs were first used by my ancestors for travel and for transporting supplies in hard-to-reach areas. Frozen rivers were like highways for the sled dogs. Until the 1960's, sled dogs were a very important part of Alaskan life. Then airplanes replaced the sled dogs for things like delivering mail, supplies and travel. There are still some remote places that use sled dogs to do those old jobs. But for my family, we train the dogs, run in competitions around the state, and host guests that want to see what it's like at a sled dog camp.

"Whoa!" exclaimed Jared. "Look at this picture." He was pointing to a very old picture of a group of mushers and their sled dogs posing in snow.

"That's a photograph of my great-grandfather with the others who helped in the Great Mercy Run back in 1925," Noah responded. "He was a member of the Tlingit tribe and started the family business in mushing and training sled dogs. I learned everything I know about this work from him."

Jared looked over at me and announced, "Hey! That's the same story Bear worked on for school."

I looked at the photograph and asked Noah, "Did your great-grandfather meet Balto?"

"He sure did. In fact, that's Balto right there," said Noah, pointing to one of the dogs in the picture. "It's awesome that you are telling that story to your class, Bear. It's an exciting story in our history."

I couldn't believe I was looking at an actual picture of Balto with the mushers and other sled dogs from the Great Mercy Run. This day was turning out to be one of the best days of my life. The only thing better than meeting a real-life musher and seeing his sled dogs would be going on an actual sled run. But I knew that wouldn't be happening with a snowstorm coming. Baxter would just have to bring us back again sometime.

Suddenly we could hear the wind blowing fiercely outside and Noah realized that Gemma had not come inside with us.

He looked concerned.

"Excuse me, kids, I'm going to go out and get Gemma. Liam, could you get our guests some hot chocolate to warm them up?"

While Liam fixed our hot chocolate, he told us a little more about dog sledding.

"Dog sleds have been helping people hunt and travel in snowy and icy weather for a very long time." Liam said. "They've been the main way to deliver everything you could imagine to towns and camps that are very far away from larger cities. Dog sleds can travel over areas where no other transportation can go."

I tried to think of what it must be like to have a team of strong energetic dogs pulling a sled I was guiding. I couldn't think of anything I'd like to do more. I wanted to ask Liam so many questions, but just then Noah came bursting through the door, covered in snow. Without Gemma.

Chapter Six – Lost

"Liam!" hollered Noah, "we need to get a team ready to go. Gemma's missing and it's a blizzard outside!"

"I'm on it, Dad!" replied Liam as he quickly stopped what he was doing and put back on his heavy winter gear.

"Can we help?" I asked Noah as he grabbed a few things and was heading out the door.

"Just stay here in case Gemma comes back," he said. "The team will take a few minutes to get ready, then we can go out and try to find her." Liam and Noah left the cabin in a hurry.

I glanced at Baxter and motioned him over. "Baxter, what should we do?" I asked. "I feel like things outside are getting worse."

Baxter assured me that we'd be okay. "Let me go out and check with Ahsoka." I opened the door to let him out. I was nervous about this situation, but I knew Baxter would know what to do. He always does.

I kept an eye out the window for when Baxter returned so I could let him back in and find out what was going on. Soon Baxter slipped in the door and told me that Gemma must have run off before the blizzard began.

Baxter said, "Ahsoka told me that she saw Gemma wander off down the path while we were taking care of the dogs earlier. She had a pretty good head start before the blizzard began, so Ahsoka was afraid that she might have lost her way."

She was nowhere in sight, and it would be dangerous for her to be out in this weather for very long.

Jared and Jillian looked really scared. I told them that Baxter would take care of us, so they didn't need to be worried.

But I had to admit that I was a little scared, too.

From inside the cabin, I watched Noah and Liam harness the dog team to the sled. They put boots on the dogs' paws.

It was fascinating how quickly they worked to get the team ready. When I did my Balto research, I remembered reading about all the steps it takes to get a dog team prepared to pull a dog sled. I was impressed at how fast Noah and Liam got it done. Before long, we could hear Noah yelling out commands to the dogs and they were off.

"Baxter, what can we do to help besides stay here and wait?" I asked. It was very hard not to do anything.

"Do you think we should use our bubble to help find her?" I asked.

"I've been wondering the same thing, Bear," said Baxter, "because we could see from above. The problem might be the visibility in the snow. It's really blowing out there and it makes it difficult to see clearly. Our magic bubble won't pop open while we're traveling in it, but it could still be hard to find Gemma in a blizzard."

I trusted Baxter and knew he wouldn't put us in danger. Finally, he agreed that we needed to try and help if we could.

Jared, Jillian, and I got our coats and snow gear back on, then followed Baxter outside. It was snowing like crazy and the wind made the snow blow sideways. I could barely see the little red dog houses just a few feet away. I wondered how we'd ever see Gemma from up in the air.

Jared pulled the bottle of Marvin's Magic Bubbles out of his coat pocket and poured some right outside the door. Baxter gathered us all around and told us to stay close. He put his nose into the sticky bubble solution and began to sniff and snuffle. Soon a bubble formed, but it quickly popped from the strength of the wind.

"You kids are going to have to squish even closer together and make a wind break around me so I can get this bubble blown," Baxter told us.

We huddled closer. Baxter tried again and this time the bubble began to grow larger and larger. It surrounded us, and we lifted off.

"Now Jared, I want you to hold on tight to Jillian. We'll be safe, but it's going to be a bumpy ride. We'll have to watch for trees in the way, because I'm going to float as low as possible. Keep an eye out below for Gemma's red coat. Thankfully, it will stand out against the snow."

I was nervous about the blizzard going on around us. It was very hard to see through the snow, which was blowing sideways and blocked the view to the ground.

"Hey, look!" hollered Jared above the loud wind, "I see Noah and Liam with the dogs down there!"

Sure enough, when I looked carefully, I could see a string of dogs pulling a sled along the road below. It was an amazing sight. I was filled with excitement, but also fearful. This must have been how the mushers on The Great Mercy Run felt as they raced to save the people in Nome.

"Baxter, what happens if we see Gemma? She won't be able to hear us through the bubble if we are calling her name. How will we be able to get her attention and help her?"

So many thoughts were running through my head. I was scared to be lost in the wilderness during a blizzard with my little brother and sister. Even with Baxter watching over us, it seemed so dangerous.

I couldn't see the dog sled team anymore. In fact, it was even harder to see below us now than it was before. I was beginning to think we'd made a big mistake. Daylight was fading, and I knew it was only a matter of time before we'd have to stop.

Jillian and Jared were being brave, but I could see the look of fear on their faces. Our adventure to Alaska was turning into a nightmare.

Baxter yelled, "Watch out, kids!" just before the bubble dropped quickly toward the ground.

Chapter Seven – The Red Coat

Our bubble jerked violently back and forth as the wind blew us around like a loose balloon. Jillian began to cry. I held my hand out toward her so she could have something to hold onto.

Before we knew it, our bubble landed with a thud in a small snow-covered clearing. Baxter popped the bubble and yelled over the fierce wind and snow. "I'm sorry to give you all such a scare, but I saw a bit of red just before we came down. It's over there at the edge of the forest. Hold on to one another so no one gets lost!"

We walked close together, trying to stand up to the strong wind that was blowing against us. I was leaning forward to keep my balance, but I was afraid Jillian wouldn't be able to walk in this wind without falling over. She clung to the back of my coat with all her might.

"Gemma!" We yelled again and again at the top of our lungs. The whooshing of the blowing snow made us sound like we were barely making a noise. It seemed impossible that Gemma would be able to hear us.

Jared pulled on my coat and I turned to see what he wanted. He was pointing towards a sloping hill up ahead. Baxter barked and led us in that direction. When we got to the place Jared had seen, we noticed it was darker where he pointed and difficult to see through the blizzard. We huddled together and Baxter yelled out to us, "I think Gemma is hiding under the pile of dead trees. That space is so small, it's going to be hard to get her out."

We hollered Gemma's name as loudly as we could. There was no answer. The daylight was quickly fading and we didn't have much time left to work.

I thought of an idea that might help Gemma, but it would mean that Jillian would have to climb under those fallen trees to see if Gemma was there. Jillian was already scared, so I was pretty sure she wouldn't want to let go of my hand to get down on the ground and climb into a dark space.

Baxter barked and got our attention. "Bear, I know what you're thinking. Jillian's the only one small enough to climb into that space and look for Gemma."

Jillian's eyes got big and started to fill with tears. She hid her face with her mittens for a moment, then wiped her eyes and nodded her head. "I can do that," she said bravely.

We all crouched down on the ground near the fallen trees. I took off my scarf and gave one end to Jillian. "Hold onto to the end of this while I hold onto the other end," I told her. I thought it would help her to know she was connected to me.

Jillian scrambled onto the snowy ground and ducked under the branches. I could hear her faintly as she yelled Gemma's name. Then I felt the end of the scarf drop loosely. She wasn't holding it anymore.

Panic filled my body and I looked up at Baxter and Jared. Had I made a terrible mistake? Now we might be missing two girls in this dangerous storm.

All we could do was try to see into the dark hole where Jillian went and holler her name. I tried to pull away at the heavy branches, but they didn't budge.

Please, God, help Jillian get out safely and bring Gemma with her if she's in there too. I prayed to myself.

From a distance we could hear dogs barking. The noise moved closer and soon we could see Noah's dog sled team leading them to where we were. I felt such a relief to know we had help.

Noah and Liam ran to the edge of the fallen trees, and I pointed into the dark space and yelled Gemma and Jillian's names. Noah grabbed a flashlight from his pack and shined it into the darkness. We waited for what seemed such a long time.

Noah waved his hand towards us and we could see that he was reaching for something. Suddenly Jillian's small arm poked out of the dark hole, and she climbed out onto the ground. Then another wonderful thing happened. We saw a figure in a red coat come out of the hole right behind her! It was Gemma. The girls were going to be okay! We hollered and smiled. The dogs barked and jumped around in celebration. Jared and I hugged Jillian while Baxter nuzzled her face. Noah and Liam were hugging Gemma while Ahsoka rubbed lovingly next to her.

I noticed the sky looked lighter because the clouds were moving out. The wind had died down too. Noah motioned us all over to where he stood. He waved us to climb on the sled. It was a tight fit, but we hung on with all our might and off we went!

The team of dogs pulled us so fast that it felt like we were floating over the snowy ground. I couldn't believe I was really riding with a dog sled team just like the mushers on the Great Mercy Run. After all the excitement of searching for Gemma, then Jillian, it felt incredible to be a part of this adventure. Oh, how I wished I could tell this story to my class. They would think I was crazy. It was a secret I could only share with Jared, Jillian, and my talking dog, Baxter. Man, oh, man. It was still the best day ever.

Chapter Eight – Going Home

When we returned to Noah's cabin, we helped get the dogs settled comfortably into their houses. We were all tired, but it was such a relief to have found Gemma and to have kept Jillian safe and sound, too.

"Noah, that was the most amazing thing I've ever done," I told him. "Riding with a dog sled team is even better than I imagined it would be."

"I can't thank you enough for helping us find our Gemma," Noah said. He hugged each of us. "You were all so brave out there. This may not have been the Great Mercy Race, but you were heroes just the same."

Gemma, who had been so quiet up until now, spoke up. "I'm very sorry I ran away. I was just mad that I'm not allowed to lead the dog team on the sled. But I know now that I'm not ready. I was so scared out there. I didn't mean to cause everyone to be in danger trying to find me. I hope you can forgive me."

"We're just so happy you're safe, Gemma," said Jared, "I'll bet one day you'll be ready to be a musher for your dog team, and maybe we can come back here to watch you do that."

Gemma smiled shyly at Jared. "I'd like that. Thank you."

We finished up the last of our hot chocolate. I looked out the window and could see that the blizzard had finally stopped. I glanced over at Baxter and he nodded his head. I knew it was time to go home.

"Noah, thank you for giving us the chance of a lifetime today," I said. "We have to be getting home now that the storm is over."

"Are you sure? Do you have far to travel?" Noah asked. "I can give you a ride to where you need to go."

It would be hard to explain that we traveled to Alaska by a magic bubble. No one would ever believe us.

Thinking fast, I responded, "We sure appreciate the offer Noah, but it will just take a few minutes to get home." I said. It wasn't a fib…exactly. True, we were far from home, but it wouldn't take long to get back there in our bubble.

After our goodbyes with Noah, Liam, and Gemma, we went outside. Baxter ran over to the little red dog houses to say goodbye to his good friend, Ahsoka. She barked a goodbye to us too.

Next we gathered at the side of the cabin where there was a nice flat spot for bubble blowing. Jared cleared off a spot on the cement and poured out some of Marvin's Magic Bubbles for Baxter. He began to sniff and snuffle. We huddled close to Baxter and soon we were up in the air and on our way back to Missouri. This was our first time floating in a bubble as it was getting dark.

"Baxter, how are we going to see to get home?" I asked.

Baxter chuckled. "No worries. It's the same as floating in the daytime. We'll just have to use our directions to help us. Do you want to get your compass out?"

I pulled out my phone and sure enough the compass aimed us right where we needed to go. This time, the only thing we could see were small lights way down on the ground. We got past Alaska, Canada, and back into the northern United States. We noticed that there were lots more twinkling lights below. I was getting anxious to be home.

"Hey, look down there!" Jared hollered. "It's like looking at stars on the ground." The tiny lights far below were beautiful.

Jillian, who was leaning on Baxter, was fast asleep. She had been such a hero today. Even though she still had a hot chocolate mustache, I knew my little sister wasn't so little anymore.

Before we knew it, I could see that we were back in our town. This magic bubble stuff was really something special.

Baxter spoke up, "Okay, kids, we're almost home. It's not as late as it seems, but it is getting a little dark." He continued, "When we get home Mom and Dad won't even know we were gone. It will be as if we've just been playing outside for a couple of hours. They won't be worried or notice anything. I'm so proud of you all for helping our new friends today. I hope you enjoyed our trip this time. Another great state, another great adventure."

Looking down, I could see our neighborhood lights and as we got closer, I could see the lamp posts shining in front of our house. "Hold on, everyone!" Baxter announced, "We're coming down."

We landed gently. Baxter nuzzled Jillian awake and popped our bubble. As we walked into our cozy warm house, put our coats away, and looked for Mom and Dad, I gave Baxter a big pat on the head and told him, "You rock, buddy. Thanks for making my dream come true today. I got to feel like a real dog sled musher and it was awesome."

Baxter wagged his tail and went to lay down on his dog bed. That dog of mine, he's the best. I can't wait for our next big adventure.

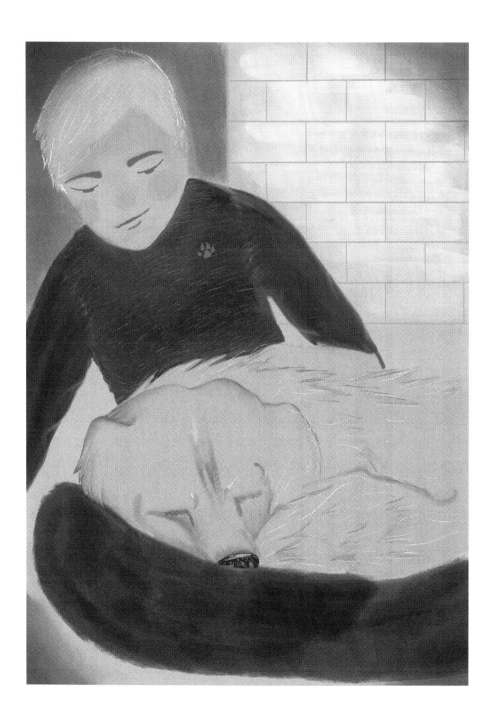

The End

Want to Learn More?

https://www.forgottenhistory.me/amazing-feats/the-great-race-of-mercy

https://kids.kiddle.co/Balto

https://wiki.kidzsearch.com/wiki/Juneau,_Alaska

About the Illustrator

For most of her life, Ashley Lynn Voltmer has been artistically expressing her thoughts and ideas. Her high school art teacher sent her to the Kansas City Art Institute at age 14 where she received invaluable training and felt very at home. She enjoys exploring different styles and media, but her current favorite medium is watercolor. Her great admiration for street art has led her down the rabbit hole of stencil making and murals, as well. During the past several years, she has been commissioned and has also sold prints of her work. Ashley loves the way art is able to bring people together and spark new perspectives in others. Becoming an illustrator is something very recent, and she believes that being a part of projects that teach and spread awareness is a very honorable position to hold.

About the Author

Paula Shue Winfrey is a publishing late bloomer. Though writing has always been a beloved hobby, her dream of writing children's books took a detour as she raised a family and spent 23 wonderful years as an elementary teacher. With many book projects in the works, she's finding time to create, enjoy grandmahood, and appreciate life.

You can contact Paula at:
stjoecpl@sbcglobal.net
https://www.facebook.com/paula.shuewinfrey
Instagram- silverliningsdecor
Twitter- Paula Winfrey@stjoecpl

Message from the Author

Thank you for taking the time to read my book.
I would be honored if you would
consider leaving a review for it on *Amazon*.

Check out these other amazing Children's Books from Paula Shue Winfrey:

Adventures of the Bubble Kids Series

COVID-19 Pandemic Series:

Because We Stayed Home

Because We Didn't Give Up

Amazing Things Press

amazingthingspress.com

Made in the USA
Middletown, DE
05 January 2022